THIS HOUSE IS HOME

WRITTEN BY
DEBORAH KERBEL

ILLUSTRATED BY
YONG LING KANG

OWLKIDS BOOKS

This is my family.

I'm Lily. That's me with
the sketchbook.

We live in the big house at
the end of the lane.

The world is a busy place.

Change rushes

this way

and that.

But Grandma says our house is old
and steady as mountains.

Last fall, two foxes with clipboards came knocking
on our door. They wanted to buy our house.

"No, thank you," Grandma said with a smile.
"This house is home, and we'll live here
for the rest of forever."

In spring, change marched over the hill and right onto our lane.

The knocking came again.

Grandma offered everyone cookies
and lemonade, then shooed
them away like flies.

The diggers arrived with summer.

Their long metal arms pulled down our neighbors' homes.

They flattened the trees and tore away all the grass.

A road appeared in the distance.

Every day, its long gray tongue snaked
toward our house, closer and closer, until it
had pushed right up to our door.

It didn't bother knocking.

And suddenly, we were an island in a river of concrete.

Then came the cars.

They sped by our windows,

this way

and that.

The rumble of wheels shook
our walls all day long.

At night, buzzing engines
sawed my dreams in half.

It began to feel like those
metal arms had pulled down
our happiness too.

Even our beautiful garden had
disappeared under a smudge of cement.

There was only one flower left.

I had to save it!

It was scary crossing the road.

Now I had to find
my flower a new
place to grow.

That night, my dreams became whole again.

The road had melted into a sea.

The cars had shrunken to fish.

My house had grown sails.

And I was its captain.

The next day, I jumped out of bed and ran to my window.

I looked down.

The road was just a road.

The cars were just cars.

Our house was still a house—
    old and steady as mountains.

  The only thing that felt different …

        was me.

As I drew, the breeze brushed
over my cheeks,

this way

and that.

The blue sky went on forever.

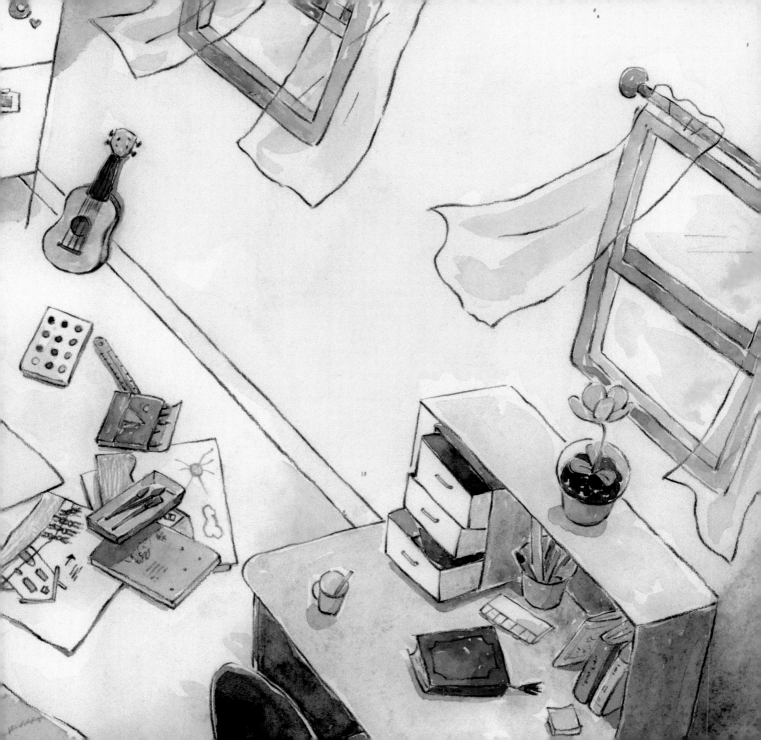

It was the perfect kind of day...

... to move mountains.

For Simone, mover of mountains —D.K.

For Eustace Ng. You are wonderful! —Y.L.K.

Owlkids Books acknowledges the financial support of the Canada Council for the Arts, the Ontario Arts Council, the Government of Canada through the Canada Book Fund (CBF), and the Government of Ontario through the Ontario Creates Book Initiative for our publishing activities.

Published in Canada by Owlkids Books Inc.
1 Eglinton Avenue East, Toronto, ON, M4P 3A1

Published in the US by Owlkids Books Inc.
1700 Fourth Street, Berkeley, CA, 94710

Library of Congress Control Number: 2020939381

Library and Archives Canada Cataloguing in Publication

Title: This house is home / written by Deborah Kerbel ; illustrated by Yong Ling Kang.
Names: Kerbel, Deborah, author. | Kang, Yong Ling, illustrator.
Identifiers: Canadiana 20200259148 | ISBN 9781771473804 (hardcover)
Classification: LCC PS8621.E75 T55 2021 | DDC jC813/.6—dc23

Edited by Debbie Rogosin | Designed by Alisa Baldwin

Manufactured in Shenzhen, Guangdong, China, in September 2020, by WKT Co. Ltd.
Job #20CB0359

A   B   C   D   E   F

 Publisher of Chirp, Chickadee and OWL
www.owlkidsbooks.com

 Owlkids Books is a division of bayard canada